**First published in the United States 1989
by Chronicle Books**

Text copyright © 1987 by Ulf Nilsson
Illustrations copyright © 1987 by Eva Eriksson

First published in Sweden 1987 by Bonniers
Printed in Denmark
Library of Congress
Cataloging-in-Publication Data

Nilsson, Ulf, 1948-
    Little Bunny at the Beach.
    [När lilla syster Kanin anin badade i det
stora havet. English]
    Little Bunny at the beach / Ulf Nilsson,
Eva Eriksson.
        p. cm.
    Translation of: När lilla syster Kanin anin
badade i det stora havet.
    Summary: At the beach Little Bunny's big
brother comes to the rescue when her playful
antics cause her to drift out to sea.
    ISBN 0-87701-610-0:
    [1. Beaches–Fiction. 2. Brothers and sisters
–Fiction. 3. Rabbits–Fiction.]
I. Eriksson, Eva. II. Title.
PZ7.N589Lg 1989
[E]–dc19   88-30841
Distributed in Canada by   CIP
Raincoast Books   AC
112 East Third Avenue
Vancouver, B.C.
V5T 1C8

10 9 8 7 6 5 4 3 2 1

Chronicle Books
275 Fifth Street
San Francisco, California 94103

Little Bunny at the Beach

Ulf Nilsson ❦ Eva Eriksson

Chronicle Books
San Francisco

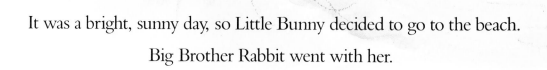

It was a bright, sunny day, so Little Bunny decided to go to the beach.

Big Brother Rabbit went with her.

Little Bunny hopped into the waves.

"Be careful," yelled Big Brother Rabbit as he shivered at the edge of the sea.

But Little Bunny didn't hear him.

She was too busy diving.

She was too busy floating.

She was having so much fun,

she didn't notice she was drifting out to sea.

Big Brother Rabbit jumped in and brought Little Bunny back to shore.

"Now, be careful," he warned.

"Humph," said Little Bunny.

And she hopped back into the waves.

"Fine," said Big Brother Rabbit.

"You can float out to sea all by yourself then."

And he marched back onto the beach.

Little Bunny looked around.

The sea looked awfully big.

It looked awfully deep, too.

"Help!" cried Little Bunny.

"Dolly's cold and scared and she's drifting out to sea!"

Big Brother Rabbit marched back into the water.

"Dolly's lucky you were there to help her,"

he said as he and Little Bunny brought Dolly safely back to shore.

Then the three of them made a special beach just for Dolly

where they splashed and swam for the rest of the day.